Time Spies
Signals in the Sky

By Candice Ransom
Illustrated by Greg Call

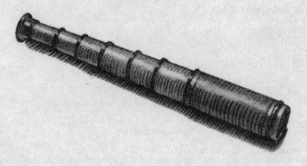

MIRRORSTONE

SIGNALS IN THE SKY

©2007 Wizards of the Coast, Inc.

Cover and Interior art by Greg Call
First Printing: May 2007

9 8 7 6 5 4 3 2 1

ISBN: 978-0-7869-4353-1
620-10987740-001-EN

Library of Congress Cataloging-in-Publication Data

Ransom, Candice F., 1952-
    Signals in the sky / Candice Ransom ; illustrated by Greg Call.
        p. cm. — (Time spies ; 5)
    "Mirrorstone."
    Summary: Whisked back to 1863 Virginia with the aid of a magical spyglass, the three Chapman children meet real-life Civil War spy, John Doyle.
    ISBN 978-0-7869-4353-1
    1. United States—History—Civil War, 1861-1865—Juvenile fiction. [1. United States—History—Civil War, 1861-1865—Fiction. 2. Virginia—History—Civil War, 1861-1865—Fiction. 3. United States. Army. Signal Corps—Fiction. 4. Spies—Fiction. 5. Time travel—Fiction. 6. Magic—Fiction. 7. Brothers and sisters—Fiction.] I. Call, Greg, ill. II. Title.
    PZ7.R1743Si 2007
    [Fic]—dc22

                                                                                    2006102200

J TIM

U.S., CANADA,	EUROPEAN HEADQUARTERS
ASIA, PACIFIC, & LATIN AMERICA	Hasbro UK Ltd
Wizards of the Coast, Inc.	Caswell Way
P.O. Box 707	Newport. Gwent NP9 0YH
Renton, WA 98057-0707	GREAT BRITAIN
+1-800-324-6496	Please save this address for your records.

Visit our Web site at **www.mirrorstonebooks.com**

To Tazman

Contents

Jefferson's Ghost

It's your fault," Alex Chapman said. "We have to do yard work because you got us in trouble."

"I did not," said his sister Mattie. "You did."

"Just because you're nine, you think you know everything," Alex said.

"Nine's better than dumb old eight—"

Alex threw a bunch of crabgrass at her. They had been weeding the rose garden all afternoon. The July sun was hot and Alex felt as crabby as the grass he was yanking.

"Please don't yell any more," said five-year-old Sophie. "You're giving me a stomachache."

"Truce!" exclaimed a new voice.

A young man in navy slacks and a striped polo shirt stood by a red rosebush. He wore his dark hair in a buzz cut. His blue eyes crinkled in the bright sun.

"Is it safe to enter the battle zone?" he asked.

"Huh?" said Alex.

"I could hear you guys fighting all the way out front," said the stranger. "No one answered the front door, so I came out back. I'll be staying at your inn tonight, but I guess I'm a little early."

"Guests come early all the time." Mattie

2

waved her hand, as if she ran Gray Horse Inn by herself. "Which room will you be in?"

"I'm supposed to be in the Jefferson Suite."

Alex exchanged a meaningful glance with Mattie. Their new Travel Guide was standing in the rose garden!

"We'll bring you some refreshments," said Mattie. "Come on, Alex."

Alex and Mattie raced up the back porch steps and into the kitchen.

"We have the Travel Guide all to ourselves!" Alex danced around the kitchen.

When his family moved from Maryland to Virginia, Alex knew he'd miss his friends. But he never dreamed that the old house, which his parents had turned into a bed-and-breakfast, would be the best place in the world to live.

What other house had a tower room with a secret panel? What other house had an old desk with a magic spyglass hidden inside? The spyglass took the kids on fantastic adventures. Whenever a guest came to stay in the Jefferson Suite, they knew their next adventure was about to happen. That guest was always their Travel Guide back in time.

Mattie poured fruit punch into a pitcher. "We might find out where he's sending us." As she set glasses on a tray, she said, "Put cookies on that plate. Make it look nice."

Alex didn't care. He was anxious to get back outside.

Sophie and the Travel Guide were sitting on the bench in the garden. Mattie set the tray on the wrought-iron table nearby.

"Are you a mailman?" Sophie asked the man.

The man laughed. "No, I'm Sergeant Frank Doyle. I'm in the army. But I'm on leave right now. So I decided to visit some historical places in Virginia."

Alex poured a glass of punch and gave it to Frank Doyle. "Where are we going next?" he asked. Then he said hastily, "I mean, where are *you* going next?"

"Monticello," their guest replied. "Thomas Jefferson's home. That's near here."

Mattie nodded. "What places have you been to already?"

"I just came from Fredericksburg. I walked around the old town and all the Civil War battlefields."

"Cool." Alex pretended to shoot an imaginary musket.

Frank Doyle sipped his juice. "When I was in Fredericksburg, I heard an exciting story about James Monroe, who was the fifth president, and Thomas Jefferson."

A story about two dead presidents didn't sound that exciting to Alex, but maybe the Travel Guide would give them a hint about their next trip back in time.

"Before James Monroe was president," began Frank Doyle, "he was a lawyer in Fredericksburg. Thomas Jefferson was his law teacher—"

Alex made a snoring sound. Sophie giggled.

Frank Doyle laughed. "Okay, I'll jump to the good part. Years later, Monroe's descendants turned his office into a museum. One winter evening—this was in the 1960s—Monroe's great-great-great-grandson Lawrence was walking down the street near the museum when he saw two men arguing. They had on Colonial clothes."

The hair on Alex's arms prickled. "Who were the men?"

"Thomas Jefferson. And James Monroe. Lawrence saw the men go up to the door of the museum and . . . walk right through it! He banged on the door until the museum guide opened it. Lawrence asked her where the two men had gone. Do you know what she said?"

Alex leaned forward. "What?"

"She said she hadn't *seen* any men. Lawrence looked around but he couldn't find them. But when he went out the front door"—Frank paused—"there was a big crack that hadn't been there before. When I went to the museum, I saw the crack in the door."

Sophie's eyes were as big as nickels. "Did you see the ghosts?"

Just then the back door opened. Mr. Chapman came down the porch steps and across the lawn. He held out his hand for Frank Doyle.

"You must be Sergeant Doyle," he said. "Welcome to the Gray Horse Inn. I'm sorry I didn't greet you."

"Your children made me feel at home," said Frank Doyle.

"He told us a story about the time Thomas Jefferson and James Monroe walked through a door!" Mattie said.

Mr. Chapman shook his head. "Since we moved here, the kids are suddenly interested in history. They tell their mother and me all these facts they've picked up somewhere."

Alex put his hand over his mouth to keep from laughing.

"So you're at Fort Gordon." Mr. Chapman sat down next to Sergeant Doyle.

"Yes sir, I'm in the Signal Corps, learning about satellite communications."

Mattie put the glasses and pitcher back on the tray. "Alex, bring the cookie plate."

Ordinarily he would have made a remark about her bossiness, but he was too excited. Sophie followed them into the kitchen.

Inside, Alex said, "Tomorrow morning we'll be off on another adventure!

I wonder what our mission will be?"

As Time Spies, they didn't simply travel back in time. They were sent back for a reason.

"I hope it's something with ghosts!" Alex said.

"You'll just have to wait for breakfast to find out," Mattie said. "He'll leave a postcard

9

like all the Travel Guides do. That'll be the hint as to where we're going."

Sometimes Mattie was so practical it got on Alex's nerves.

— 2 —

A Surprise
in the Attic

Alex was dreaming about being able to walk through doors when he heard somebody tapping on *his* door. He sat up in bed, wondering if ghosts could make sounds.

"Alex!" Mattie whispered. "It's me."

Alex got out of bed and opened the door. Mattie padded in, dressed but barefoot.

"Is it time for breakfast?" he asked. Breakfast was served at eight on the dot.

"Not yet," Mattie replied. "I couldn't sleep."

"So you woke *me* up?"

She lowered her voice. "I heard something in the attic!"

The Jefferson Suite and the tower room were on the third floor. But over some of the second-floor family bedrooms was a small attic. No one had ever been in it.

"Do you think it's a ghost?" Alex asked eagerly.

"I hope not!" Mattie said. "Come with me to look."

She went out in the hall while Alex dressed in shorts and a T-shirt. As Alex and Mattie tiptoed past Sophie's room, her door swung open.

"Where are you going?" she asked, clutching her stuffed elephant Ellsworth.

"To the attic," Alex said.

"Me and Ellsworth are coming too!"

They crept to the end of the hall. A rope dangled from the ceiling. Alex grabbed the rope and pulled hard. A trapdoor opened and a set of stairs dropped down. Alex climbed up first. At the top of the steps, Alex let his eyes adjust to the dim light slanting through the single window. A bamboo folding screen and a wooden trunk stood near the window.

"Do you see a ghost?" Mattie asked from behind him.

"No, but look!" Alex pointed to the trunk. "A treasure chest! I bet it's filled with money and jewels!"

He ran over to the trunk. Sophie and Mattie hurried after him.

Alex lifted the lid. Instead of jewels or gold coins, all he saw was a bunch of musty old fabric.

"Clothes!" he said in disgust, pulling out old shirts, pants, boots, and dresses. "Nothing but crummy clothes. Yuck!"

Mattie picked up a long cotton print dress. "This is pretty. Soph, this one's your size. Here are some boots. Let's try them on."

She and Sophie ducked behind the screen, and then came out wearing the long dresses and old-fashioned boots.

"It's fun wearing this stuff," Mattie said. "Alex, put on the pants and shirt."

"No."

"You're chicken." She made *cluck-cluck* sounds.

"Who are you calling a chicken?" Snatching up a pair of pants, a shirt, and boots, he stomped behind the screen and changed into the old clothes.

Then he clomped out and said, "What is

the big deal about these old clothes—"

Mattie gripped his arm. "Alex! The time!"

"Oh, no! I bet it's after eight o'clock!"

"Hurry!" Mattie said, clopping down the steps.

They peeked into the dining room. It was empty. Alex heard the sound of running water in the kitchen. His parents were cleaning up.

"We missed breakfast!" Mattie said. "And the Travel Guide! What'll we do?"

Alex spied the postcard in the silver tray on the sideboard. He darted into the dining room, snatched the card, and ran back out again.

"Come on!" he said, clattering back upstairs to the third floor.

Alex pushed on one edge of the book-case and the secret panel swiveled inward. He crawled through the passage. Sophie

15

and Mattie followed behind him, dragging their long skirts. Mattie closed the bookcase panel.

Alex sat on the floor in the tower room. He held out the postcard to show Mattie.

"Weird," Mattie said. "I hope we're not going to be climbing again!"

"Read the words," Sophie said.

Mattie flipped the card over and read:

> Dearest Sister, I have seen the elephant. Our brother is missing again. Yours, J—

"What's 'J'?" asked Sophie.

"Never mind," Mattie said. "Get the spyglass."

Alex opened the secret panel on the desk and removed the spyglass from its velvet-lined box.

"Wait!" Mattie said. "We can't go like this."

"Why not? We always go back to the olden days," Alex reminded her.

Mattie shook her head. "We may still be dressed wrong. Let's change."

Alex frowned. Mattie was so bossy!

"You made us put this stuff on! And you

made us late," he said. "I'm going like this. You can stay here!"

"You know the spell won't work unless we all go," Mattie said.

Sophie tugged on Alex's arm. "Please don't fight!"

"Are we going on this trip or not?" He held out the spyglass. Sophie gripped the middle with one hand.

Mattie blew her bangs upward. "If we're dressed wrong, it'll be *your* fault."

"Take the spyglass!"

His sister took the other end of the spyglass. The spyglass grew warm under Alex's fingers. Glowing designs of stars and moons suddenly appeared on the brass tube. Whirling colors sparkled behind his eyelids.

Whoosh!

His feet slid through a tunnel of flashing lights.

As Alex fell through time, he had only one thought. He was *still* mad at know-it-all Mattie.

— 3 —

The Wig-Wag Station

Alex opened his eyes. He was standing on a grassy hilltop. Birdsong filled the soft air. Before he noticed anything else, Mattie and Sophie appeared beside him.

"Where are we?" Mattie asked.

"How should I know?" said Alex. He was still miffed at his sister.

He looked around and saw an enormous old oak surrounded by a ring of tree stumps.

The raw, splintered wood told him that the trees hadn't been cut down long ago. Two white canvas tents had been pitched in the clearing. A couple of horses grazed nearby, tied to pickets. Firewood was laid in a shallow rock pit.

"Is this a campground?" Mattie asked.

Alex shook his head. "I don't think so. I wonder why they cut down all the trees except that great big one?"

"Maybe they needed wood," said Mattie. "Whoever *they* are. Where are they?"

Sophie pointed up. "There."

Alex looked up. The lower and middle branches of the huge tree had been chopped off. The upper branches supported a wooden platform. A second, higher platform nestled in the very top of the tree.

"What a cool tree house!" he exclaimed.

"How do we get up there?"

Sophie went around the back of the tree. "Here's the ladder."

Alex and Mattie followed her. A tall, crudely made ladder stood propped against the tree trunk.

Alex tested the bottom rung. "Come on. Our mission isn't on the ground."

"How do you know?" asked Mattie.

"Where else would it be?" said Alex, and began climbing.

Sophie slipped Ellsworth in the pocket of her apron and set off after Alex.

"Why are all of our missions way up in the air?" Mattie complained. "I went up the pea vine and rode that gigantic Ferris wheel. Now I have to go up this shaky ladder!"

Alex was too busy climbing to answer. The ladder must have been thirty or forty feet tall. At last he reached the top and scrambled onto the wooden platform. The platform was bare except for a shorter ladder leading to the higher platform.

Sophie and then Mattie tumbled onto the platform. Mattie groaned when she saw the second ladder.

"I refuse to move," she said, lying flat on the wooden floor.

Just then they heard loud flapping sounds, like the wings of a prehistoric bird. The sound came from the upper platform.

Alex bolted for the ladder. "I hope it's a giant bird and we can ride it!" He had always wanted to go to the Amazon and see the strange creatures of the rainforest.

Sophie and Mattie were right behind him.

When Alex reached the top of the ladder,

he stopped and stared. A man in a dark blue uniform stood on the platform. He held a long wooden flagpole pointed upward. A large white flag with a red square in the center was attached to the pole.

As Alex watched, the man briskly dipped the flag to one side twice, snapping it to the upright position. Then he dipped it in front of him three times.

"Alex, will you move?" came Mattie's voice. "I don't want to stand on this ladder all day, you know."

Jerking the flag, the man gawked at Alex. His brass buttons glinted in the sunlight. Alex realized the man was wearing an old-fashioned army uniform.

"Get up here," the soldier ordered.

Alex hopped up on the platform. Then he turned and helped Sophie over the ledge. Mattie's head popped up next. The soldier took Mattie's hand and hauled her over the edge.

"Are there more of you?"

Mattie blinked. "Huh?"

Dark hair fell across the soldier's forehead. He flicked it back with one hand and fixed his sharp blue eyes on Alex. "The rebels must be hard up, recruiting such clumsy young spies."

"We're not spies," Alex said, crossing his

fingers behind his back. They *were* spies, in a way, but not rebels—whatever that meant.

"Then who are you?" asked the soldier, setting the flag down near a folding camp stool. "And where are you from?"

"Uh—" said Alex.

This was always a sticky moment when they traveled back in time. They had to be careful not to reveal that they were from the future.

Mattie spoke up. "I'm Mattie. This is my brother, Alex, and our sister, Sophie."

"And this is Ellsworth," Sophie said, holding up the stuffed elephant.

Smiling, the soldier shook Ellsworth's foot. "You're mighty far from the jungle."

"We're from—Virginia," Alex said, hoping they hadn't landed in the middle of Massachusetts or something.

26

But the soldier nodded. "Since we're *in* Virginia that isn't hard to figure out."

Alex glanced at Mattie. They still were in Virginia. But what year?

"I'm Private Doyle," said the soldier. "You may call me John."

"How come you're waving that flag?" Mattie asked.

"I'm a wig-wagger," John replied. "A signalman in the U.S. Army Signal Corps. I was sending a message to another signalman."

Alex gazed out over platform rail. The steep hill dropped down to a dirt road. On the other side of the road, thick woods grew for miles. Where was the other signalman?

John sat down on the stool and took two objects from a canvas haversack. One was a small notebook. The other was a spyglass!

27

Alex's heart raced with excitement. Was John's spyglass magic too?

Propping his elbows on his knees to steady the spyglass, John peered through the eyepiece. Then he wrote something in the notebook.

"What are you doing?" Alex asked.

"Receiving a reply."

Alex squinted into the distance. "I don't see anybody."

"He's on the next hilltop," said John. "I can only see him through the spyglass."

"Is this your house?" Sophie asked.

John laughed. "No, but I feel like I live here since Dan—that's my partner—got sick. Luckily, he should be back tomorrow."

He put the notebook and spyglass in a small canvas bag. Then he twisted the flagpole until it came apart in two sections. He rolled the flag and stowed it and the poles in a long canvas sack, fastening the sack with leather straps.

"Let's go," he said.

Alex scurried down the ladder first, followed by Sophie and Mattie. John shouldered the bags and climbed down last. When they reached the ground, he lit the firewood with a match and set a frying pan of bacon on the fire.

"Now tell me the truth," John demanded. "Who are you?"

"I'm Alex and—"

John cut him off with a stern glance. "How do I know you aren't spies?"

"Because we're kids," Mattie said.

"Anybody can be a spy," said John. "Women, children. Secret messages are even smuggled in dolls." He looked at Sophie's elephant.

"Ellsworth is just a toy," Alex said.

"There's a war on, sonny boy," John said.

"War?" Alex gulped. Which war?

"Are you three refugees from Fredericksburg?" John asked.

Alex remembered the story the Travel Guide had told them, about Jefferson and Monroe's ghosts walking through the museum door. That was in Fredericksburg. What else had the Travel Guide seen there? Battlefields! The Civil War!

"Did you lose your home in the battle last winter?" John asked.

"Yes," Mattie said quickly. "We were going to our aunt's house but our horse ran off."

They had used that story before and it had worked.

"I love horses," said Sophie.

John smiled at her. "You remind me of my sister when she was your age." He turned the bacon with a fork. "My brother and I are closer. We were born a year apart. He and I used to love to sing together."

"What songs?" Sophie asked.

"We used to sing 'Yankee Doodle.' I'd sing a line, then he'd sing a line and so on." He began singing:

"Father and I went down to camp
Along with Captain Gooding
And there we saw the men and boys
As thick as hasty pudding."

"You sing good," Alex said. "What happened to your brother?"

John gazed into the flames. "Wesley and I both joined the U.S. Army and became signalmen. But then the war began. I stayed with the Union, but Wesley joined the Confederate army. We had an argument the day he left."

"Why would brothers fight on different sides?" said Alex.

"We're from Maryland, near the Pennsylvania border," John replied. "Most people there side with the Union. But some are Confederates."

Mattie frowned. "I don't understand."

John looked at her in surprise. "Are you sure you're Virginians? Did the shelling addle your brains?"

"Yes," Alex said. "We have—what is it? Magnesium?"

Mattie rolled her eyes. "He means we have *amnesia*. We can't remember why we're fighting this war."

"The Southern states didn't like the Northerners telling them how to run their governments. So they broke away from the Union in the north and formed their own country:

The Confederate States of America. The president didn't want the United States split apart. A war began." John stared at them. "Do you remember the year?"

Alex shook his head. "We don't know where we are, either."

"It's 1863," John said. "We are on Mount Pony, several miles from Fredericksburg. After the battle in December, General Robert E. Lee—he's head of the Confederate army—kept his troops in Fredericksburg. The Union army is just across the Rappahannock River."

"How come you're not over there with the Union army?" Mattie asked.

"I sometimes work behind enemy lines."

Mattie touched John's blue wool sleeve. "What color is your brother's uniform?"

"Gray," John replied sadly.

Sophie said, "I bet you miss your brother."

John sighed. "Yes, I do. Being in this war is hard. But the worst part is not knowing where Wesley is. The last I heard he was near Fredericksburg, but that was ages ago. I'm afraid I may never see him again."

This time Alex elbowed Mattie. He knew their mission. They had been sent back to help John find his brother.

— 4 —

Codes and Key Words

The purple twilight had deepened to night. An owl hooted in the woods.

Alex shivered and stretched his hands to the fire. "Can we stay with you?"

John's face looked serious. "Just for tonight. If I am caught harboring the enemy, I could be arrested."

"We're not the enemy," Mattie insisted.

"You live in Virginia," said John. "Virginians

35

are Confederates. Rebels. That makes you the enemy."

"We live in Virginia, but we think war is wrong," said Alex.

"I believe you. I think war is wrong too, but I must serve my country." He pulled out a watch on a chain and snapped it open. "I have to send a message."

"How can anybody see the flag at night?" Mattie asked.

"I'll show you."

John picked up the tubelike bag and canvas haversack, slinging both over his shoulder. He began climbing the ladder. Mattie followed, and then Sophie. Alex went last, glad the fire cast light on the rungs. When they reached the top platform, John unpacked the bags.

Instead of taking out the flag, he removed

two copper tubes and one of the staff sections. He set up one of the copper tubes by the rail. Then he clamped the other copper tube onto the staff.

"What's all that?" Alex asked.

"This is a flying torch," John explained. "The one by my feet is a foot torch. The cylinders are filled with turpentine."

He slipped the copper disks around the flying torch. "These keep the flame from overheating the copper." He lit one end of the torches and flames shot skyward.

John stood behind the foot torch, holding the staff upright at his waist. Then he dipped the torch to the left, returning it to the upright position before dipping to the right. He repeated the motions.

"I'm telling the other signalman a message is coming," he said.

Alex watched intently. The torch inscribed lines across the sky, like writing with sparklers. But John was not writing. He was sending a message using the same signals he made with the flag.

"What's the other torch for?" he asked. He was thinking about becoming a signalman in the army. They got to use such neat equipment!

"The foot torch gives the other signalman a fixed place to look," John replied.

Mattie looked out across the dark forest. "Can't other people see that light?"

"Like the enemy? Yes, they can. But I'm not sending a very important message. It's not in code." He stopped and dipped the torch to the front three times. "That's the signal my message has ended." He snuffed both torches with copper end caps.

"Look! There's a tiny little light!" said Sophie. "Like a firefly."

John laughed. "That 'firefly' is the other signal officer answering me. He is actually miles away." He looked through his spyglass, and then nodded. "Message received. We can go down now."

He packed up his equipment and they climbed back down the ladders.

"It's late," John said. "You three can sleep in my partner's tent."

The tent was small, with only one bedroll. Mattie and Sophie shared the blanket.

"Alex." Mattie's voice floated out of the dark. "I don't get all this North and South stuff. We haven't studied the Civil War in school yet."

"I know," he said. "But we're in the middle of it. I wonder where the armies are? So far we've only seen John."

Mattie didn't answer. She and Sophie were already asleep.

Alex found an extra blue wool jacket. He pulled it over him and went to sleep, flags waving in his mind.

A moan woke Alex. He sat up, blinking. Morning light streamed through the tent flap.

He threw off the uniform jacket and hurried outside. John lay beside the fire. His face was flushed and his teeth chattered.

"I've caught my partner's fever," he said weakly. "I'm too dizzy to climb the ladders today."

Alex had an idea.

"We'll send the messages," he said. "Mattie and me. We can learn."

"Absolutely not," said John. He tried to get up but fell back. "Well, maybe."

"Yes!" Alex said eagerly. He leaned into the tent and yelled, "Wake up! We have to fix breakfast and get to work!"

Mattie and Sophie crawled out. With John's directions, the kids cooked bacon and corncakes over the campfire. After breakfast, it was time for their signal lesson.

"You'll have to work as a team," John said to Alex and Mattie. "Mattie, you're the tallest. Take the flag from the bag and join two sections of staff."

Mattie followed his instructions. When the flag was put together, she held it at her waist. "It's heavier than I thought."

"You're ready to wig-wag," John said. "Dip the flag to your left. Now bring it back into position. Smartly! You can't take too long between moves or the message will be garbled."

"What can I do?" asked Alex. After all, it was *his* idea. Now Mattie was going to the send the messages!

John reached into the haversack and pulled out a leather-bound book. He handed it to Alex. "This is the signal book. It has the two-element signal code we use."

Alex opened the book eagerly. Inside were two columns. The letters of the alphabet ran down one side of the page. In the next column, numbers had been written beside each letter.

"'A equals one-one,'" Alex read aloud. "'B equals one-two-two-one.' What does it *mean*?"

"The numbers one and two are the two parts of the code," said John. "One means you dip the flag to the left. Two means you dip to the right. It's a very simple system."

Mattie held up the flag. "What's 'B' again, Alex?"

He checked the book. "One-two-two-one."

She dipped the flag to the left, then to the right twice, then back to the left. "How's that?"

"Good," John said. "At the end of each word, wave the flag to the ground in front of you."

Mattie spelled her name, this time ending with the front motion.

"Don't you worry someone will see the message?" Alex asked.

John nodded. "Sometimes we use a keyword with a substitution cipher to keep the enemy from reading our messages. But we don't need one now because we're pretty far from the rebels."

Alex realized there was more to being a signalman than he thought.

John checked his pocket watch. "It's time to send the message."

"What do I say?" Mattie asked.

"My daily check-in message. It's written in my logbook. Don't forget to end with three fronts. That says the message is over." John turned to Alex. "You look through the spyglass and receive the message. Mattie writes it down." John marked a page in his logbook, and then slipped it into the haversack. "Good luck. Come down if you have any trouble."

Alex and Mattie hurried to the ladder. Alex carried the large flag bundle. Mattie looped the haversack over her shoulder. Sophie stayed with John.

At the top, Alex unpacked the bags. Mattie assembled the flag while Alex pushed the camp stool close to the platform's edge.

Then Alex read John's message in the

book. "We're supposed to send, 'Any news?' "
Flipping to the code, he began calling out the signals. "One-one, two-two—"

"Not so fast!" Mattie said, hitting herself in the face with the flagpole.

"You're supposed to go fast. Or the message won't be right."

When the message was sent, Alex peered through the spyglass. He scanned the distant hilltop until he spotted a clearing. A white flag with a red square waved at him!

"Here comes the answer," he said. "Two, one, two. One, two. Two, one, one, two. Two, one."

Mattie wrote down the numbers, and then looked at the alphabet. "The first word is 'our.'"

Back and forth dipped the flag. Alex's eye watered from squinting. But he was determined to get all the words right. When the flag finally ended with three fronts, Alex put down the spyglass.

"Okay, that's it," he said. "Let's go show John. It may be important!"

They scrambled back down the ladders with the logbook. John was sitting up. He looked a little better.

"News?" he asked.

Alex read the message aloud. "They said: 'Our cavalry is going up to give Johns and his men in the Shenandoah a smash. They may give Fitz Lee a brush for cover. Keep watch of any movement of infantry that way that might cut them off.' "

"This is very important," John said. "You two did good work."

"Do you know Fitz Lee?" asked Alex. "And Johns?"

John shook his head. "General Fitzhugh Lee is a Confederate cavalry general. The Shenandoah Valley is hundreds of miles from here. Johns is probably Joseph Johnston, another Confederate general." John flicked his hair off his forehead.

Just then Alex heard the sound of a horse's hooves. Someone was heading into camp.

"Get out of sight!" John ordered them.

There was no place to hide but behind the big oak. Alex scurried around the far side of the tree. Mattie and Sophie squeezed in beside him.

Alex peered around the side of the trunk.

— 5 —

Blinking Blinds

A Union soldier on horseback trotted into camp.

"Dan Acorn," John called. "I caught your fever."

That must be John's partner, Alex thought.

"I hope you're well enough to travel," said Dan. "We've got orders to move to a new signal station."

"Where?" asked John.

"Down the Rappahannock. South of Fredericksburg."

Alex remembered John saying the Rappahannock River separated the two armies. He wondered if it was far away.

John and Dan began packing up the camp. Dan took down the tents while John stowed their gear into saddlebags.

"We can't let John leave," Mattie whispered. "How will we ever complete our mission?"

"How can we stop him?" Alex asked. He felt a quiver of fear.

The men finished packing the equipment into canvas bags, and then strapped the bags behind the horses' saddles.

"Ready?" Alex heard Dan say.

"I'll have to take it slow," said John. "I'll follow with the packhorse."

"You know our location," Dan said, climbing

into the saddle. "See you before nightfall." He wheeled his horse and they clip-clopped down the hillside.

"He's gone," John said loudly.

Alex, Mattie, and Sophie crept out from behind the tree.

"Thanks for not leaving us," Alex said.

"I couldn't abandon you children in this wilderness," John told them. "I'll see you back to Fredericksburg, but then I have to get to my new station."

"Why aren't you staying at this one?" Mattie asked.

"Signal stations change locations to stay ahead of troop movements," John replied. "We relay messages for miles, so all the stations move at once."

John adjusted the knapsacks on the pack-horse, making room on the saddle. "My new station is south of Fredericksburg. I'm drop-ping you three off near the town."

Alex realized the Confederate army was in Fredericksburg. At first he felt afraid. Then he remembered the Travel Guide's story. Maybe they'd see a ghost!

"Let's go." John picked up Sophie and settled her onto packhorse. Then he started to help Mattie swing up.

"I'm okay," she said. "I've had a few riding lessons."

"Alex, you're riding with me." He climbed into the saddle of his own horse, and then pulled Alex up behind him.

They set off down the hill, John leading the packhorse by long leather reins. Soon they reached the main road. Woods grew on either side of the dirt road. Alex didn't see any houses. After a while he began to notice fields of stubby stumps. The ground was deeply rutted.

"Was there a battle here?" he asked.

"Yes, last winter," John replied over his shoulder. "The rebels cut down the trees to make room for their tents. The wheels of their wagons and cannons made a muddy mess."

The ugly stumps stretched for miles. The land looked scarred, Alex decided, the way his knee looked from the time he fell off his bike.

After riding for what seemed like years, John eased back the reins and said softly, "Whoa, boy."

The horse stopped and he climbed off. John lifted Sophie down from the packhorse.

"Fredericksburg is down the road about a mile," he said. "You'll probably see rebel guards sooner."

Mattie slid off the packhorse. "You're leaving us?"

"I've gone too far into enemy territory as it is," said John. "You'll be fine. After all, it's your home."

"Oh, yeah. Thanks a lot." Alex dropped to the ground with a thud.

"Take care. And hope this war is over soon." John swung up into the saddle, took the packhorse's reins, and disappeared into the woods.

"Now what?" Alex asked when John had gone.

"We get to work on our mission," said Mattie. "John said his brother Wesley might be in Fredericksburg. Maybe we can find him."

They walked down the road. Sophie held one of Alex's hands and clutched Ellsworth with the other. Soon they spotted two men in gray uniforms standing on either side of the road. They carried rifles.

One of the men jumped in front of them and ordered, "Hold it!"

The kids stopped.

"What business do you have in town?" the guard asked.

"We live there," Alex replied.

The man stepped back. "Go on, then."

Alex walked past the guards, heart thumping. That was close! Now they could see houses and more soldiers in gray uniforms.

"This place is crawling with the enemy," he said to Mattie.

Mattie tossed her hair. "They may be Confederates, but they're still Americans, same as John. Same as us."

Alex believed her, but Fredericksburg was a scary town. Holes had been blasted in the sides of brick houses. Chimneys had toppled into yards. Some houses had cannonballs stuck in the walls. Bricks and stones littered the cobblestone streets. Trash and mud were everywhere. The corner of a tattered flag poked out from the mud. Alex could see one star.

Confederate soldiers were everywhere. But the kids also saw women in wide, swinging skirts picking their way through the rubble. Children and dogs ran through the streets.

"Nobody's paying any attention to us," Mattie said. "You were right about these clothes. Where should we look for John's brother?"

"How about James Monroe's house?" said Alex.

"He wouldn't be *there*," Mattie said scornfully.

"No, but the ghost might be."

"We're on a mission, Alex!"

"I want to see the ghosts." When a soldier walked by, Alex said, "Excuse me. Do you know where James Monroe's house is?"

The soldier nodded. "President Monroe's office is on Charles Street. Up that way. Next to the cemetery."

"Thanks." Alex headed in the direction the man had pointed.

"This is a big waste of time," Mattie said. "That Lawrence guy saw those ghosts in the 1960s!"

"Maybe they came out other times," Alex said. "It won't hurt to check it out."

They turned on to Charles Street. An unpainted, one-story house stood next to a cemetery. Slatted blinds hung in a broken window.

"Monroe's office doesn't look like much," Mattie remarked.

But Alex was watching a man sneaking

along on the opposite side of the street. The man stood out because he wasn't wearing a uniform. Instead, he wore patched brown pants topped by a grubby brown jacket. A battered felt hat was pulled low over his eyes.

Instantly suspicious, Alex tugged Mattie and Sophie behind a shed.

"He's going into Monroe's office," he said.

The door latched shut. A few seconds later, an old-fashioned coffeepot appeared in the window. Alex figured the man had set it on the windowsill.

"I guess he lives there," said Mattie. "But if he's going to make coffee, why doesn't he put the pot on the stove?"

Just then, a hand took the coffeepot from the window.

Next, the slatted blinds opened and closed, opened and closed.

"Can't the guy make up his mind?" Mattie asked, sounding annoyed.

Alex's heart did a cartwheel. The window blinds were blinking in *code*. The man inside was sending a secret message!

— 6 —

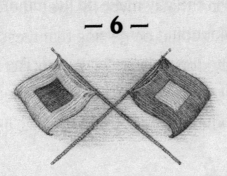

The Secret Line

That guy is sending a message!" Alex exclaimed. "He's using a code!"

"Then he has to be sending it to some-one," Mattie said. "Someone who can see that window."

Alex whirled around. Behind the shed was a wooden house. One wall was scorched black as if it had been in a fire. Bare windows stared out like empty eyes. No blinds flicked a reply.

"I don't think anybody lives there," said Alex. "Who could be getting that message?"

"They don't have to live right across the street," Mattie said. "They could be watching the window through a spyglass, like John does."

The blinds stopped blinking. The kids waited, but the man didn't come out.

"Let's go exploring," said Alex. "Maybe we can find the place he was signaling."

They followed a steep street down to a waterfront. A wide river rushed between wooded banks.

"This must be the Rappahannock River," said Mattie.

Several men in Confederate uniforms sat on upturned wooden boxes. Four men played cards so intently that they didn't notice the kids. The fifth man stood at the water's edge.

"Howdy," he said, stroking his bushy brown beard.

"Howdy," replied Alex. Looking across the river, he saw three men in blue uniforms. "Hey! Those are Union soldiers! You'd better duck!"

"What for?" asked the gray-coated soldier.

"Aren't they the enemy?" asked Mattie.

"We've been watching each other all winter," said the man. "They won't shoot."

Alex frowned. "I'm confused."

"So are we, son, most of the time." The man grinned through his beard. "We won't shoot until there's a battle and the generals can't seem to make up their minds when that'll be. In the meantime, we look at each other."

Sophie tugged on the soldier's gray sleeve. "Is your name Wesley?"

"Nope. Name's Zachary."

"I'm Sophie. And this is Mattie and Alex." She held up her elephant. "This is Ellsworth."

Zachary tipped his hat. "Pleased to meet you."

"Were you in that big battle that was near here last winter?" asked Alex.

"Yup. It was something. I finally saw the elephant."

"What elephant?" Sophie asked. "Ellsworth and me want to see him."

Zachary chuckled. "It's an expression. It means you've been in the hottest fighting. But now the armies are stuck with the river between them. That's good if you're on picket duty, like me."

"Why?" asked Mattie.

"I'll show you." Zachary cupped his hands around his mouth and yelled, "Hey, Billy Yank! Got some coffee?"

"Johnny Reb! Only if you got some salt," yelled one of the Union soldiers from across the river.

"Your name isn't Johnny Reb," said Alex.

"And his isn't Billy Yank," said Zachary. "They're just nicknames."

He bent down and placed a small cloth bag on a toy-sized, flat-bottomed boat. String ran from the boat's mast to a wire stretched over the river. Zachary tugged on a pulley and set the boat sailing across the water. When it reached the other side, the Union soldier took the sack of salt, put a paper-wrapped object in its place, and turned the boat around.

Alex waded into the shallow water and retrieved the little boat. Zachary unwound the paper-wrapped bundle to find a packet of coffee and a ribbon-tied cloth roll that contained scissors, needles, and thread.

"Ah! He gave me a housewife, too," Zachary said in delight.

"You mean that sewing kit? What do you need that for?" asked Mattie.

"In case I have to sew a button on my uniform." Zachary waved at the Union soldier, who waved back. "We've been trading supplies all winter. He's a good man."

"Will you have to shoot at him when you start fighting again?" asked Alex.

Zachary sighed. "I hope not."

Suddenly Alex felt sad. "We'd better go. It's getting dark."

"Come back and keep me company any time," Zachary said to them.

As they walked downriver, Alex said, "He's nice."

"So is John," said Mattie. "They are just people who have to fight. The war isn't their fault."

"I'm hungry," said Sophie. "And tired."

Alex was hungry, too. But he didn't know where they would find food. Or where they'd sleep.

Down the river, he saw a blue heron take off from a mudflat. The bird flapped its great wings as it soared over the trees. Then Alex saw something else: a light tracing a line in the sky.

"Mattie!" he exclaimed, pointing. "That's a flying light! I bet it's John's new signal station."

She stared at the light. "But it's on the other side of the river. How will we get over?"

"We could make a boat," he suggested.

With a stick, Sophie poked at something at the water's edge. "Look."

Alex and Mattie ran down the bank. Sophie had discovered a rowboat, half-concealed in the brush.

"I'd ask for a million dollars, but I know now that doesn't work," said Mattie.

"Let's hope the boat does," Alex said, pushing the boat into the river. He stepped into it. "Come on. It only leaks a little."

Mattie helped Sophie in, and then climbed in herself. She pulled a pair of oars from under the seat and gave them to Alex. He fitted the oars into the locks on the sides of the boat and splashed them into the water. The boat scuttled back toward the shore.

"We're supposed to be going *across* the river," Mattie said.

"It's not that easy!"

He tried again. This time the boat spun in a circle. Then he dipped the oars instead of splashing and the boat headed in the right direction.

On the other side of the river, they climbed

out of the boat. They waded in the shallows to shove the boat up on the bank beneath a low-hanging willow tree.

"Look for the flying light," Alex said. "That's where the signal station will be."

"There!" Sophie pointed up at a streak of light.

Alex led the way downriver. It was fully dark now. He stumbled over rocks. Sharp twigs scratched his face.

At last they came to a small clearing. A man was sitting in a tree, peering through a spyglass. A lantern hung from one branch and a flying-light torch lay on the ground beneath the tree. The torch had been snuffed out.

"John!" cried Sophie, bounding ahead.

The man jerked the spyglass. "Sophie? Is that you?"

"And Alex and Mattie," said Alex.

"Well, I'll be—" John climbed down the tree. "How did you get here?"

"In a boat." Alex pointed back toward the river. "Is this your new station?"

"They all aren't fancy like the one on Mount Pony," said John. "Are you hungry? I've got leftover beans and biscuits." He dished out food from a pan over the glowing coals of a campfire.

Alex had never tasted anything so good. "Your biscuits are better than my mother's."

"Glad to hear it," said John. "But you should be at home with your mother. You could be in danger."

"What danger?" asked Mattie.

"Something is in the air," John replied. "I don't know exactly what, but it's big."

A *battle*! Alex thought. Then he told John about the sneaky man, the coffeepot in the window, and the blinking blinds.

"The sneaky man you saw is probably a Confederate agent. The coffeepot was a signal that meant that he was going to transmit a message with the blinds."

"If we see that man again, we'll follow him," said Alex.

John shook his head. "He'll be hard to find. I bet he's sending messages along the Secret Line."

"The Secret Line? What's that?" Mattie asked. She looked down as if she expected to see a line on the ground.

"It's not a real line," John answered. "It's the route Confederate spies use to smuggle information from Washington, D.C., to Richmond. They've found that using the rivers is the safest way."

"Does the Rappahannock River go to Washington?" Alex asked.

"No, but it eventually runs into the Potomac River. Washington is built right on the Potomac River, you know."

"Do the spies use rowboats?" Alex said. He wondered if they had taken the sneaky man's rowboat.

"Rowboats, fishing boats, anything." Suddenly John trained his spyglass across the river.

A light appeared in the darkness.

"That's the window of somebody's house," said Mattie.

"Hey, look!" Alex pointed at an arc of light swinging from a rooftop in the town. "Another flying light!"

"John, what does that mean?" asked Mattie.

John angrily flipped his hair from his eyes. "That was the *same* message I just sent! It must be from a rebel signalman!"

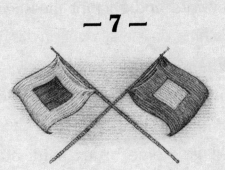

Double Agents

Across the river, the flying torch was put out. Then the signal light from the window disappeared.

All was dark once more.

"The Confederates are watching this station," John said grimly.

"It's probably that spy," said Alex. "The sneaky man."

John sighed. "Whoever it is, we'll have to

use a keyword and encrypt messages from now on."

Just then Sophie yawned hugely.

"You children should be in bed," said John.

"We'll go home," Alex said, standing. "Come on, Matt. You too, Soph."

"Good night," John said, as they left his camp. "If you need anything, send a message to Frank. He's the picket—the guard—along the river. I'll tell him you three can be trusted."

"Thanks," Mattie called back. To Alex, she said, "Where are we going? We don't have any place to sleep."

"Yes, we do," he replied. They had reached the willow tree. Pulling back the leafy curtain, he revealed the shadowy hump of the boat.

"We're sleeping in the boat?" asked Sophie.

Mattie sighed. "It's better than nothing."

She and Sophie lay down at one end.

Alex slumped in the other end, but he couldn't go to sleep. As stars winked above him, he thought about the sneaky man in James Monroe's office building. If that man was the spy stealing John's messages, how would they catch him?

One of the stars fell in a white streak. A shooting star. It reminded him of the ghost messages left by a flying torch. An expression flitted into his head: You have to fight fire with fire. Then an idea struck him like the falling star.

Alex dozed off, picturing himself in a trench coat and an old-fashioned hat half-covering his face.

We're going to do *what*?" Mattie asked the next morning, as they trudged through town.

"Become double agents," Alex replied in a hush-hush tone. "The best way to catch a spy is to *be* a spy."

They had awoken at dawn. After washing in the chilly river, they rowed the boat back over to the Confederate side. Alex led the way back into town.

"So you want us to spy for both sides?" Mattie asked.

Alex had it figured out. "See, we're really spies for John—the Union army. But we'll *pretend* to be spies for the Confederate army to help John catch that sneaky guy."

"Who's going to believe a bunch of kids are spies?" Mattie asked.

"Anybody can be a spy," Alex told her. "Remember what John said?"

"Okay," Mattie said. "So where are we going now?"

"Back to Monroe's office. We can pick up the sneaky man's trail there."

When they got to Charles Street, it was deserted. They hesitated at the corner of the Monroe building. No coffeepot stood in the window. The blinds were shut.

"What should we do?" asked Mattie.

Alex shrugged. "We can't peek in the window to see if he's there."

"Knock on the door," said Sophie.

Alex looked at his little sister. Sometimes she had the best ideas of all. He strode up to the door and knocked. His heart knocked almost as loudly against his ribs. What would they do if the spy answered the door?

Before he could think up a story, the door swung partly inward.

A figure hung back in the shadows. "What do you want?" said a low voice.

"We're—uh—" Alex stammered.

"We're here to help," Sophie said. "We're spies too."

The man peered out at them, especially at Sophie and Ellsworth. He opened the door wider and said, "Come in."

When they were inside, he slammed the door behind them.

Alex's blood chilled. They were trapped! Had he made a mistake?

It was the sneaky man, all right. He wore the same brown pants and jacket. The battered felt hat lay on a table, next to a notebook and pencil. The only other furnishings in the room were a rickety chair, a lantern, and the coffeepot. A haversack had been tossed in one corner.

Now that Alex could see him up close, he noticed the man had blue eyes and dark hair.

And he was kind of young.

"Who sent you?" the man demanded.

"Nobody," Mattie replied. "We came by ourselves."

Without warning, the man suddenly snatched Ellsworth away from Sophie.

Sophie howled and lunged at him.

"Hey!" Alex exclaimed. "Give that back to her!"

Ignoring them, the man pulled a knife from his belt and held it over the elephant, preparing to plunge it into Ellsworth's back.

"No-o-o-o-o-o-o-o-o!" Sophie's scream was loud enough to stop both armies in the middle of a heated battle.

"What do you think you're doing?" Alex jumped up to smack his hand away.

The man whirled out of his reach. "Take it easy. I'm just getting the message."

"Are you crazy?" Mattie yelled. "What message?"

But Alex understood. He remembered John talking about messages being smuggled in dolls.

"Wait!" he said. "There isn't any message hidden in that."

The sneaky man raised one doubtful eyebrow. "Messages cross enemy lines in rag dolls all the time."

"Not this time," Alex said.

The man handed Ellsworth back to Sophie, who clutched her elephant.

"You're a bad man!" she said.

The sneaky man flipped his long dark hair out of his eyes. "No, I'm not. Not really."

Alex swapped a glance with Mattie. She nodded slightly. Only one other person flicked his hair like that—John!

Taking a deep breath, Alex said quietly, "You're Wesley."

The man looked at him sharply. "How do you know my name?"

"We're here to help you find your brother. He's right across the river."

"What brother? What are you talking about?"

"You *are* Wesley Doyle, aren't you?" Mattie asked. "Your brother John isn't too far from here."

"We saw him just last night," Alex added.

The man glared at them. "I don't believe you. Why would my brother—if I had one—talk to some rebel young'uns?"

Sophie spoke up. "Because he's a lot friendlier than you are!" She was still furious that Ellsworth had nearly been stabbed.

The man's eyes narrowed. "Tell me

something about this man that makes you think he's my brother."

"Well," Mattie said, "you both have dark hair that you flip out of your eyes."

The man snorted. "I need a haircut, that's all. Not good enough." He sat in the rickety chair. "You're not leaving this place until you tell me what you're really doing here."

"We're here to help you find your brother!" Mattie said angrily. "You're too stubborn to find him yourself, just because you had that big fight—"

The man was on his feet, towering over Mattie. "How did you know about the fight I had with my brother? You *are* spies! Sent to bring me out in the open!"

"No, we aren't," said Alex. "Honest."

He realized that they could talk for days and the man would not give in. They needed real proof to convince him.

Alex thought back to the night around the campfire on Mt. Pony. An idea formed in his mind. It *could* work.

He went over to Sophie, who cradled Ellsworth.

"Sophie," he said. "You have to do something very important."

"What?" She was instantly suspicious.

"You know how everyone has to be brave in a war?"

She nodded.

"I want you to give me Ellsworth. It's *her* turn to be brave."

– 8 –

Ellsworth's Mission

Sophie's eyes grew round. "What does she have to do?" she whispered, still clinging to her stuffed elephant.

"She's going to carry a message, okay?" Alex replied. It was the only way to convince Wesley that his brother was just over the river.

"She won't be hurt, will she?" Sophie asked, loosening her grip on Ellsworth.

"Nothing we can't fix." Alex held out his hand. "Okay, Soph? Will you let Ellsworth go on this mission?"

Reluctantly, Sophie gave him her most precious belonging in the world. "Okay. But she'd better not get hurt!"

Alex turned Ellsworth over and examined the seam down the elephant's back.

"Do you have a sewing kit?" he asked Wesley.

"Sewing kit? Oh, a housewife."

The spy dug through the haversack on the floor, pulling out a flannel bundle tied with a ribbon.

Alex untied the ribbon and unrolled the flannel. Inside he found a needle, thimble, thread, and a pair of tiny silver scissors. He picked up the scissors and started to cut into Ellsworth's back.

Sophie leaped forward. "What are you doing?"

"Just a little surgery." He looked at Mattie. "You do it. I'll write the message."

Mattie deftly picked out the threads in the elephant's seam while Sophie watched nervously.

"May I borrow some paper and your pencil?" Alex pointed to Wesley's notebook and pencil lying on the table.

"Help yourself."

Alex tore a strip off a piece of paper and wrote: *Father and I went down to camp*. He folded the paper into a small square.

Mattie held out Ellsworth. "Is that big enough?" She had ripped a two-inch seam in the elephant's back.

"Yeah." Alex poked the note inside. "Sew it up, okay? Not too tight?"

Mattie nodded and threaded a needle from Wesley's kit.

She sewed the opening closed with large, loopy stitches.

"Like this?" she asked.

"Perfect." Alex knew John would see the big, sloppy stitches and know there was something inside the elephant.

He took Ellsworth and headed toward the door.

Wesley blocked his exit. "Where do you think you're going?"

"If you want real proof, you have to let us go to the river," Alex said.

Wesley's hard blue eyes softened. "All right. But I'm going with you."

He opened the door and checked up and down Charles Street. Then he pushed Alex, Sophie, and Mattie onto the walk.

He slipped out and locked the door.

"This way," Alex said. He headed down the steep cobblestone street.

As they approached Zachary's campfire by the river, Wesley stopped.

"That's a picket post," Wesley said.

"Yeah, but they're gone," said Alex. "They use something we need."

Across the river, a lone Union picket paced back and forth.

That must be Frank, Alex thought. He hoped John had talked to Frank about them.

"Be quick about it," Wesley said, ducking behind a bush. "Don't say a word."

Alex ran to the water's edge.

Yes! The little trading boat was on this side.

He put Ellsworth in the little boat, and then tugged on the rope-pulley to launch it into the river.

The boat breezed to the other shore. Alex watched as Frank bent down to pick it up.

He crossed his fingers. If Frank threw the elephant away, his plan would fail. Not to mention the fact that Sophie would start another war!

But Frank looked directly at Alex.

Alex couldn't say a word, not with Wesley hidden right next to him. So he pointed downriver, toward John's signal station.

Frank nodded, waving Ellsworth in a broad arc. Then he climbed the bank and vanished into the woods.

"Ellsworth!" Sophie whimpered.

"She'll be okay," Mattie said. She shot Alex a loaded glance.

Alex hoped the Union soldier understood.

"What now?" Wesley said, still hidden.

"We wait," said Alex.

Wesley stretched out under his bush, his hat tipped over his eyes. Alex knew he was not asleep. If they tried to escape, Wesley Doyle would catch them as quick as a lizard.

After a while, the rope bounced like a guitar string. Alex sprang up. The Union soldier was sending the boat back!

"Is Ellsworth on it?" Sophie asked anxiously.

"Yes!" Alex breathed a sigh of relief.

Sophie splashed into the water, reaching the boat before Alex. She grabbed Ellsworth with a cry and hugged her.

Alex waved his thanks to the picket on the other side of the river. Then he said to Sophie, "I need to see if Ellsworth completed her mission."

She handed over her elephant. Using his fingernail, Alex plucked the loose threads from Ellsworth's back. The paper was still there, but in a different spot. He pulled it out.

Wesley appeared at his side. "Hand it over."

Alex gave him the paper.

Wesley unrolled the slip and read, flicking his dark hair out of his eyes. Then he looked at Alex.

"You're telling the truth. This is my brother's

handwriting," he said. "And only he would know he sang the first line of 'Yankee Doodle' and I sang the next line."

He showed the paper to Alex and Mattie. Underneath Alex's printing, someone had written: *You sing*: "*Along with Captain Gooding*." Beneath that, the person had added: *Meet me at my station after dark*.

"He wants to see you!" Mattie said to Wesley.

"It's dangerous. I'll have to go through enemy territory." Wesley's voice grew soft. "But I haven't seen my brother in two years."

Alex felt a lurch of excitement. They had almost accomplished their mission! In just a few hours, the brothers would meet again. And he and Mattie and Sophie could go home.

To avoid being seen, they all waited in the

shelter of a willow tree until it was fully dark. Alex sat on an anthill and was bitten several times.

"I don't want to be a spy anymore," he said, scratching the bites. "It's a lot of sitting around and waiting."

"It's also bad food. Not enough sleep. Cold. Rain. Broiling sun." Wesley ticked the items off on his fingers. "But this is how I serve my country."

Mattie stared at him. "*Our* country. We're all Americans. Like your brother."

Wesley sighed. "I told John to come over to this side, but he wouldn't. He's stubborn."

"Funny," said Alex. "He told us *you* were stubborn."

They were silent for a while. A silvery moon rose over the trees and a bullfrog croaked on a log.

"It's time," Wesley said, parting the willow curtain. "Where is your boat?"

"Down by that big rock," Alex replied, showing the way.

Wesley pushed the boat into the water. "Get in."

The kids stepped in the boat as he fitted the oars into the locks. Alex noted that Wesley was a much better rower than he was. The oars sliced quickly through the ink-black water. On the other side, Wesley hauled the boat up on the bank.

"The signal station is this way," Alex said to him.

"I know where it is," said Wesley. "I saw the flying light last night."

"Did you copy that message?" asked Mattie. "John was really mad."

Wesley didn't answer.

He walked through the woods barely rustling a leaf. Alex, Mattie, and Sophie crashed through the bushes like a pack of moose.

At last they came to the clearing. But no one was perched in the trees. And no one waited on the ground. The campfire was cold.

Wesley wheeled on Alex. In the moonlight, Alex could see the anger in the man's eyes.

"You tricked me! I knew I shouldn't have believed you!"

"It's no trick!" Alex said. "You saw the note. Only John could have written the second line of the song."

"It's not Alex's fault John isn't here," Mattie said.

But Wesley wasn't listening to her. He turned his head toward the woods.

Then Alex heard boots cracking twigs, a lot of boots. And the jingle of metal.

Wesley whirled back to face them. "Thanks to you three, I am now in enemy territory! Be perfectly still—"

They could see dark blue uniforms through the black trees. Union soldiers! Hundreds of them! The men marched down a road on the other side of the woods. The

strip of trees hid the kids and Wesley from view.

Alex froze. No wonder Wesley was furious. It looked as if they had led him straight into a trap.

As he stared into the darkness, he saw a shadow detach itself from the men. The shadow gave a low whistle. Alex recognized the first line of "Yankee Doodle."

Next to him, Wesley stiffened. Then he whistled the second line of the song.

John Doyle dashed into the clearing. He clasped his brother in a bear hug. Wesley hugged back. The two men did not speak.

Alex knew they couldn't. If they were caught, they would both be arrested.

Suddenly a voice yelled, "Private Doyle." The soldier sounded closer than he was, Alex realized. "Doyle! Go to your post *now*!"

John stared at Wesley. Alex knew John needed to talk to his brother. But he had to obey orders too.

"What are we going to do?" Mattie whispered urgently.

Alex looked at her. They had done it before. How hard could it be to do it again?

The Flying Light

Where's your stuff?" Alex asked, looking around for John's equipment.

John spoke in a low voice. "The station was moved again. Why?"

"We're going to send the messages," Mattie replied.

"Absolutely not!" John said. "It's my duty."

"You and Wesley need to talk," Alex said. "This may be your only chance."

In the silence that followed, a breeze ruffled the treetops. A raggedy cloud passed over the moon.

"Doyle!" the voice bawled from the darkness. "Get back to your post!"

"Where's the new station?" Alex asked. "If we hurry, no one will see us."

"It's a house, just through the woods," John replied. "The station is on the widow's walk. The ladder is at the back and the equipment is already up there."

Alex didn't know what a widow's walk was, but John was already handing him his small canvas bag.

"Be careful," he told Alex. "And . . . thanks."

"We'll meet you back here," Alex said with more confidence than he felt. What if they couldn't find the house? What if the Union soldiers caught them?

Grabbing Sophie's hand, he headed into the woods. Mattie was close on his heels. The bluish black figures still marched along the road in an unending line. Alex used the woods as a screen. He could see through the curtain of branches, but he and Mattie and Sophie were well hidden.

Soon they stumbled on a rutted lane. At the end of the lane stood a three-story house. A ladder leaned against the back wall.

"This must be it. I'll go up first," Alex said.

At the top, the slate roof slanted up toward a small railed platform. *The widow's walk*, Alex thought, crawling on his hands and knees across the smooth slates. Once on the platform, he found the stool, the lantern, and the canvas bag with the flags and torches.

"Come on!" he called down to Mattie and Sophie.

When they were all crowded in the tiny space, Alex lit the lantern. Then he undid the straps on the canvas bag and began assembling the flying light.

"We're getting a message," Mattie said.

In the distance, a single light blazed. Just above the single light, lines of light traced arcs in the dark sky.

Mattie propped John's spyglass on the railing and called out the signals. Alex wrote them down in John's notebook.

"Urgent message," he read back. "Need new keyword." He looked at Mattie. "We don't have the new keyword."

"Why didn't John tell us a keyword?" said Mattie.

"I guess he forgot. And we don't have time to go back and ask him." He watched the distant signal flash three-three-three. The signalman was waiting for their reply.

"What should we do?" Mattie asked.

"If we don't reply with something, they'll know we've taken over John's post and he'll get in trouble."

"Ellsworth," said Sophie.

"Soph," said Alex. "Now is not a good time to talk about Ellsworth."

"The *word*," Sophie insisted. "Don't you need a word?"

Alex finally understood. "*Ellsworth* as the keyword! Brilliant, Soph."

Mattie grabbed his arm. "If we send 'Ellsworth,' the enemy will figure it out too. They're probably watching."

"Wesley has been spying on the Union signalmen," said Alex. "Right now he's too busy."

Alex slid the flagstaff through the brackets on the torch and tightened the screws. Then he picked up the flame shield, but dropped the copper disk. It slid down the slate roof. He held his breath as he stretched out to retrieve it.

"Hurry!" Mattie said.

"I am!" He lit the wick of the flying torch. "Okay. Fire away."

"I'm the signaler," Mattie said.

Alex gripped the torch. "It's my turn!"

"Please don't—" Sophie began.

"You're right, Soph," Alex said. "This is no time to fight." He held out the torch to Mattie.

"No, it's your turn." She read from the notebook, "Two, one. One, one, two. One, one, two."

Alex dipped the torch left and right. When he had spelled *Ellsworth*, he flashed three-three-three. "I hope the other signalman got it."

"Alex," said Mattie. "How do we figure out what the guy is saying back?"

"I don't know," Alex replied. "We'll just have to write down the code as we see it, and then ask John to translate it."

A few minutes passed, then a distant light flared across the sky. Mattie peered through the spyglass while Alex wrote down the code. When the signalman flashed three-three-three, the kids stopped.

As Alex called out the code numbers, Mattie scribbled them down in the notebook. When the message ended, Alex snuffed the flying light with the copper cap, and then took the torch apart.

"Let's go," he said when the torch and staff were bundled in the canvas bag. "Bring the notebook. We have to show the message to John." He left John's equipment on the floor of the widow's walk, but shouldered the small haversack.

On the ground, they followed the lane back to the woods. No blue-black figures marched up the road.

"Let's use the road," Alex said. "It'll be faster."

They found John and Wesley sitting on a log, talking. The men sprang up when Alex and the others ran into the clearing.

"What happened?" John said. "We saw your lights."

"We received a message," Alex said, giving John the canvas bag. "We wrote it in your notebook. But we can't figure it out."

"I didn't give you a keyword!" John said.

"We made one up," said Mattie. "*Ellsworth*."

"Ellsworth! I should have guessed. And I didn't tell you how to decipher incoming messages." John took the notebook and began writing.

Wesley spoke. "I know you can't tell me the message. But I'd like a hint."

"A big battle is coming," John said finally. "Probably tomorrow. Our troops are moving tonight."

Alex drew in a breath. John just told a secret to the enemy! Then he realized Wesley wasn't the enemy, but his brother. John might never see him again.

Alex thought about Mattie. Even if they'd had the biggest fight in the world, he wouldn't want to leave his sister without saying good-bye.

"This is it," John said sadly.

"Yep." Wesley sounded sad too.

John put on his cap. "I'll see you, little brother."

"Not unless I see you first." Wesley gave a jaunty salute.

The two men walked out of the clearing in different directions. John hurried up the road toward the signal station. Wesley hustled down to the river.

The kids helped Wesley push the boat into the water. They all climbed in and Wesley rowed across the river with sure strokes.

"What's going to happen?" Alex asked when they reached the other shore.

"I suspect John will finally see the elephant," Wesley replied, hiding the boat in a clump of reeds.

Mattie waded through the chilly water. "What about you?"

Wesley's short laugh sounded like a bark. "Me? I've already seen the elephant."

On the bank, he turned to them and said, "Thanks. It meant a lot seeing my brother."

Then he disappeared into the bushes, like an animal vanishing into its den.

"Where is he going?" Sophie asked.

"Back to the war." Mattie nudged Alex. "What now? I suppose you want to hang around for the big battle."

Alex dug his toe in the dirt. Normally he would be itching to see the cannons and horses and armies. But what if he saw John and Wesley? He couldn't watch brother fight brother.

"No," he said. "Let's go home."

Mattie nodded as he pulled the spyglass from his pocket. They clung to its familiar wood-and-brass shape.

Alex closed his eyes as colors spiraled and whirled. He felt himself falling through a light-filled tunnel.

Thud.

His clunky boots hit the floorboards of the tower room. Sunlight streamed through the tall windows. It was no longer night in a war-torn land, but a bright, cheerful morning in the Gray Horse Inn.

"I'm starving," Mattie said.

"Me too," said Alex. "Next time we have an adventure, let's eat breakfast first!"

As he put the spyglass back in its velvet-lined box, Mattie opened the second secret panel in the desk and took out a letter sealed in an envelope.

"I can't wait to find out what happens to John and Wesley," Mattie said. "But first, let's get out of these clothes. My boots are soaking wet."

"I thought we were going to eat first," Alex complained.

Mattie shook her head stubbornly. "The

attic is closest. Change first."

"Food."

"Clothes!"

Alex remembered John and Wesley. He held up his hands in a time-out sign. "Truce?"

"Truce," Mattie agreed. "Let's take the letter to my room first."

She pivoted the bookcase panel and crawled through on her hands and knees. Alex followed her. But Sophie was not behind him. He turned around.

"Soph? What are you doing?"

"Nothing."

Alex thought he saw Sophie drop a fragment of cloth into the drawer—red and white with a little blue.

He blinked. Maybe it was all those flying-light signals making him see things that weren't there.

Dear Mattie, Alex, and Sophie:

On this trip, you traveled back to the most difficult time in America's history.

The Civil War, which lasted from 1861 to 1865, ripped apart our nation. For years before the Civil War, our country was divided by territory. The northern states were above the Mason-Dixon Line, a boundary between Pennsylvania and Maryland. These states were also called "free states" because slavery was outlawed. States below the Mason-Dixon Line allowed slavery. The North and South couldn't agree on issues involving slavery and states' rights.

Then Abraham Lincoln became president in 1860. He was against slavery. His election caused the Southern states to break away from the United States. Eleven southern states formed their own government, the

Confederate States of America.

Richmond, Virginia, was named the Confederate capital. Washington, D.C., remained the United States capital. Because the two cities were only a hundred miles apart, most of the fighting occurred in the South. Sixty percent of the battles were fought in Virginia.

You noticed war scarred farmland, woodland, cities, and towns. People in war-torn areas suffered hardships. Daily necessities like paper, food, cloth, and soap were scarce. After a battle, many people were left homeless.

Both the Union and Confederate armies employed spies (men and women) to gather information. Some women spies became famous. Seventeen-year-old Belle Boyd revealed Union military secrets to Confederate general

"Stonewall" Jackson. Elizabeth Van Lew lived in Richmond but was loyal to the North. She sent baskets of eggs to Union generals with messages hidden in hollow eggshells.

Signal stations often moved to stay ahead of the action of the two armies. They were located on hilltops, in open fields, on top of houses, and even in trees. Other signal sites were more permanent. The station on Mt. Pony, at Culpeper, Virginia, was used by both armies during the war.

Signalmen and spies relayed information that helped generals decide when to stage a battle, like the one you heard about. On December 13, 1862, the Union and Confederate armies clashed at Fredericksburg, a town halfway between Washington, D.C., and Richmond. Confederate general Robert E. Lee and his troops won the battle. The

Union army fled back across the Rappahannock River. The two armies faced each other again during the winter of 1863. Between battles, soldiers on both sides traded goods, using homemade boats.

In the spring of 1863, the armies collided at Chancellorsville, near Fredericksburg. This was the "big battle" that everyone was waiting for. Once again, Lee won. But he lost his brightest general, "Stonewall" Jackson. After that fight, the armies headed north to a little town called Gettysburg, Pennsylvania. Lee lost the battle. From then on, the Confederates began losing the war.

On April 9, 1865, Lee surrendered his army to Union general Ulysses S. Grant. After four years of fighting, the war was over and more than 600,000 men were dead.

So what happened to the Doyle brothers? John finally "saw the elephant" at Chancellorsville. He and Wesley continued to fight on different sides throughout the war, but both survived. I'm proud to be John Doyle's great-great-grandson.

Your next adventure will be really different. Alex, you'll get your wish about ghosts!

Yours in Time,
Frank Doyle

On this mission you learned how to send messages with flags. Both armies used the Signal Corps. "Wig-waggers" and men who operated a new machine, the telegraph, could send and receive messages much faster than riders on horseback. Their work was often dangerous. Night signaling with torches made the signalman a target for enemy sharpshooters.

The two-element code worked for both signal flags and the telegraph. Flagmen motioned with their flag right or left, using an alphabet consisting of "one" and "two" combinations. Telegraph operators used a "dot-dash" version of the same code. "A," which is 1-1, would be two flag waves to the left. Telegraph operators would tap

the telegraph key twice, making a dot-dot
sound.

    Suppose you need to contact one of
your friends and you can't talk? You could
try using this code!

WHAT YOU NEED:

A pencil   A white handkerchief

A flashlight   A broom

WHAT YOU DO:

1. Tie the handkerchief to the pencil.

2. Write out your message.

3. Figure out the message using the two-element code below.

4. Send your coded message. Remember to dip your flag to the left for "1." Dip the flag to the right for "2." Dip your flag to the front once between words. And dip your flag to the front three times to sign off.

5. For night signaling, tape a flashlight to a broom handle.

TOP-SECRET TWO-ELEMENT CODEBOOK

Here is the two-element code used by the Signal Corps in the Civil War:

A = 11	N = 22
B = 1221	O = 12
C = 212	P = 2121
D = 111	Q = 2122
E = 21	R = 122
F = 1112	S = 121
G = 1122	T = 1
H = 211	U = 221
I = 2	V = 2111
J = 2211	W = 2212
K = 1212	X = 1211
L = 112	Y = 222
M = 2112	Z = 1111

TIME SPIES

"A time-traveling mystery . . . that will keep kids turning the pages!"
—Marcia T. Jones,
co-author of *The Bailey School Kids*

Give an important message to General Washington in
Secret in the Tower

Catch a dinosaur thief in
Bones in the Badlands

Climb into the pages of *Jack and the Beanstalk* in
Giant in the Garden

Help legendary magician Harry Houdini in
Magician in the Trunk

Reunite a Civil War spy with his brother in
Signals in the Sky

Unmask the Headless Horseman in
Rider in the Night
AUGUST 2007

Save the Race of the Century in
Horses in the Wind
NOVEMBER 2007

For more information visit:
www.timespies.com